An Innocent Little Murder

Other plays by the same author in English

A brief moment of eternity, A Cuckoo's nest, A hell of a night, A simple business dinner, A Skeleton in the Closet, All's well that starts badly, An innocent little murder, At the bar counter, Back to stage, Backstage Comedy, Bed and Breakfast, Blue Flamingos, Casket for two, Cheaters, Check to the Kings, Christmas Eve at the Police Station, Christmas Eve at the Police Station, Comedies for 4, Comedies for 7 or more, Crash Zone, Crisis and Punishment, Crisis and Punishment, Critical but Stable, Déjà vu, Enough is Enough, Ethan and Eve, EuroStar, False exit, Family Portrait, Family Tree, For real and for fun, Four stars, Fragile, Handle with care, Friday the 13th, Friday the 13th, Gay friendly , Happy Dogs, Heads and Tails, Him and Her, Him and Her, How to get rid of your best friends, In flagrante delirium, In lieu of flowers..., Is there a critic in the audience?, Is there a pilot in the audience?, Is there an author in the audience?, Just a moment before the end of the world, Just like a Christmas movie, Killer Sketches, King of Fools, Last chance encounter, Like a fish in the air, Lost time Chronicles, Lovestruck at Swindlemore Hall, Ménage à trois, Miracle at Saint Mary Juana Abbey, Music does not always soothe the savage beasts, Neighbours'Day, New Year's Eve at the Morgue, Nicotine, Not even dead, Of Vegetables and Books, Offside, One marriage out of two, One small step for a woman, one giant leap backward for Mankind, Open Hearts, Open Hearts, Pentimento, Perfect In-laws, Preliminaries, Quarantine, Reality Show, Running on empty, Save our Savings, Sidewalk Chronicles, Special Dedication, Stage Briefs, Stories and Prehistories, Stories to die for, Strip Poker, Surviving Mankind, The Costa Mucho Castaways, The Deal, The Fishbowl, The House of Our Dreams, The Jackpot, The Joker, The Perfect Son-in-Law, The Performance is not cancelled, The Pyramids, The Rope, The Smell of Money, The Tourists, The Way of Chance, The Window across the courtyard, The Worst Village in England, Traffic Jam on Graveyard Lane, Welcome aboard!, White Coats, Dark Humour

JEAN-PIERRE MARTINEZ

An Innocent Little Murder

English translation by
Anne-Christine Gasc

La Comédiathèque
comediatheque.net

Characters

Alan
Eve
Emma

This play can be adapted for 2 men and 1 woman
by swapping the characters' genders.

*You must obtain the authorisations from the
author prior to any public performance, whether
by professional or amateur companies :
https://comediatheque.net*

© La Comédiathèque
ISBN 978-2-37705-442-8

Act 1

A bo-ho living room looking well lived-in. A mobile phone left on the ground rings in the empty room. Alan enters, visibly preoccupied. His hands are covered in blood. He looks at the phone but doesn't pick up.

Alan – Ah shit …

The mobile phone stops ringing. Alan takes a handkerchief, delicately picks up the mobile phone and drops it in his pocket. He quickly tries to tidy the room a little. He picks up a blood-stained shirt off the ground, and examines it, aghast.

Alan – Oh no, this isn't happening...

The doorbell rings. He stuffs the shirt under a sofa cushion. The doorbell rings again.

Alan – Coming!

He disappears from view to open the door and returns following Eve, his wife.

Eve – I'm sorry, I locked myself out again. Nothing's going right today. I was assigned a legal aid case, a woman accused of murder. You're going to love this. A DIY enthusiast who cut up her husband in three pieces with a jigsaw. And you won't believe… *(She stops when she notices Alan isn't listening.)* Are you sure you're alright? Still thinking about the subject of your new play?

Alan – I am actually, but that's not the problem…

Eve – You're scaring me. What's wrong? Don't tell me your mother's coming to dinner?

Alan – No, no, don't worry…

He sits on the sofa.

Eve – Then it can't be that bad. Speaking of dinner, what do you want to eat? I don't really feel like cooking anything… We could order sushi and eat watching telly?

Alan – Yes… Well, no… I'm not really in the mood, actually.

Eve – I wasn't aware one had to be in the mood to scoff down a couple of tuna rolls… *(She sits next to him on the sofa and kisses him.)* It's not like I'm asking you to shag me senseless, right now, on the living room carpet. *(Seeing his lack of enthusiasm)* Right… Maybe later then… I'll order two dinner menus. At least with sushi there's no risk of food getting cold…

Alan – Unlike dead bodies…

Eve is visibly surprised when she hears the morbid reply.

Eve – Right… You can tell me all about your problems while we wait for the delivery, and I'll do my best to rekindle your spirits… *(She takes her mobile and calls the restaurant.)* Oyster or plum?

Alan – What?

Eve – The sauce, for your sushi! Do you want oyster sauce or plum sauce?

Alan – Yes…

He gets up from the sofa and paces around the room.

Eve – One of each, then… *(To the person on the phone)* Yes, home delivery. Two California menus. Yes, 9 Dudley Gardens… So, one oyster and one plum. Very well, thank you… *(She puts her mobile away.)* Half an hour… Come, sit next to me. Mummy will make it all better… *(She moves a cushion to make room for him and sees part of the blood-stained shirt sticking out. She pulls out the shirt.)* What the hell is this? What happened? *(Noticing the blood on his hands)* Are you hurt?

Alan – No, I… It's not my shirt, and it's not my blood either…

Eve – Whose blood is it, then?

Alan – Eve, listen, I think I may have killed someone…

Eve *(in disbelief)* – You think you…? What are you talking about?

Alan – No, I mean… I don't think… I'm sure I did…

Eve – Alan, this doesn't make any sense. People don't go around killing other people. Look at me for instance. I've often wanted to kill your mother but I've never done it. You know why?

Alan – No…

Eve – Because I'm not a killer, that's why! I don't act impulsively. I think things through. I measure the pros and the cons. And I conclude that, all things considered, twenty years in prison would be too high a price to pay for the fleeting pleasure of strangulating your mother.

Alan – Evidently, men find it more difficult to put things in perspective.

Eve – Listen Alan, I work with criminals all day at the Old Bailey, and believe me, you don't have the profile at all…

Alan – That's what I thought too… Until earlier today.

Eve – It's the subject of your new play!

Alan – Pardon?

Eve – The story of a woman who comes home from work, and her husband tells her he killed her lover? You want to know what I think of your idea, right?

Alan – For fuck's sake Eve, I killed someone, do I have to spell it out for you?

Eve – You keep saying that, but you don't get to just call yourself a killer… You have to prove it.

Alan – I do…?

Eve – You have no idea how many people confess to crimes they didn't commit. Just last week, I was defending a Boy Scout accused of murdering a priest. You're not going to believe this, but half a dozen other scouts were claiming they did it too… I had to fight the other lawyers to convince the judge that my client was the guilty one.

Alan – I see… And how did you do that?

Eve – Quite easily… My client was the only one who knew under which tree the holy man's body was buried.

Alan – So?

Eve – So? Where is the body?

Alan – He's in the next room, in the kitchen.

Eve appears to suddenly grasp the gravity of the situation.

Eve – In the kitchen? You're not serious…

Alan – Why don't you have a look?

Eve looks in the direction of the kitchen, hesitates, but doesn't go.

Eve – But… What happened? Never mind… Who is it?

Alan – It's… Patrick.

Eve – Patrick?

Alan – Patrick.

Eve – Oh no… Not Patrick …

Alan – You were hoping for someone else?

Eve – Oh my God, Alan… Tell me this isn't true…

Alan – I'd love to… Unfortunately…

Eve – It's joke, isn't it?

Alan – You're holding his shirt. Look… It's his initials on the cufflinks.

Eve looks at the cufflinks, aghast.

Eve – PS…

Alan – Patrick Sanchez. Also, he's the only one we know who wears cufflinks other than on his wedding day.

Eve – But Alan… I mean… Why?

Alan – It was an accident…

E v e – An accident? You mean… like a household accident?

Alan – Something like that, yes…

Eve – Well, go on! You were trimming the hedge in the garden, didn't see him peeing in the bushes and you cut off his… carotid? If it's anything like that, no need to worry, it wouldn't be considered a crime. With a good lawyer…

Alan – Yeah, no, it didn't happen exactly like that…

Eve – So how did it happen then?

Alan – It was more like… manslaughter.

Eve – What do you mean?

Alan – We had a talk.

Eve – A talk? You mean an argument?

Alan – Yeah, sure… An argument…

Eve – You had a violent argument, and then…?

Alan – Violent enough for me to kill him. Hang on, I feel like I'm already under interrogation.

Eve – I'm sorry… Pure force of habit.

Alan – In any case, I killed him.

Eve is crushed.

Eve – And it's all my fault…

Alan – What?

Eve – Well, indirectly, but still…

Alan – How is it your fault?

Eve – I won't let you down, Alan. Crimes of passion have a low conviction rate, you know.

Alan – A crime of passion? Do you mean… do you think that… Patrick and I?

Eve – You killed him because I slept with him, didn't you?

Alan (*bewildered*) – You slept with Patrick?

A moment of hesitation.

Eve – That's not why you killed him?

Alan – I didn't know you slept with him!

Eve – Oh, it was a long time ago…

Alan – How long ago?

Eve – I can't even remember… Maybe six months… give or take…

Alan – You call that a long time ago… Next you'll tell there's a statute of limitations?

Eve – It was… an accident.

Alan – But of course… a household accident?

Eve – It wasn't even an affair, Alan… It was only one time. I wasn't even in love with him…

Alan – Oh good, I feel much better already… Knowing my wife sleeps with men she doesn't love.

Eve – Not men! Just Patrick, I swear. It was a misunderstanding! I mean, Patrick! Seriously, can you see me with Patrick!

Alan – Steady, don't forget he's my best friend.

Eve – Don't forget you killed him…

Alan – So how did it happen, then?

Eve – It was… a misunderstanding.

Alan – I see… A sort of accidental adultery…

Eve – Exactly!

Alan – I've never heard a more fucked up excuse. Is that your legal defense strategy?

Eve – Hang on, let's each stick to our roles. You committed a crime, not me. So now you're the one who's going to have to deal with the police.

Alan – Because you're planning on calling the police?

Eve – Why, what do you suggest we do?

Alan – I was planning on calling the police. Until now. But now that I know Patrick is your lover… no one will believe the accidental manslaughter theory!

Eve – So this is my fault? And stop calling him my lover. We only slept together once!

Alan – Doesn't matter, it will still look like revenge. Premeditated, too. I'm going away for life!

Eve – We'll tell them…

Alan – What, about your accidental adultery?

Eve – Hey! At least I didn't kill anyone!

A beat.

Alan – So, what do we do?

Eve – What do you mean, we?

Alan – I thought we were in this together? You cheat on me with my best friend, and after I kill him you'd wash your hands of it?

Eve – But you didn't know I slept with him when you killed him!

Alan – Let's not split hairs.

Eve – Actually, why did you kill him?

Alan – It's really stupid.

Eve – I'm listening…

Alan – Well… Okay… So he said he really didn't like my last play.

Eve – Your last play? *Hiroshima*?

Alan – Okay, maybe it wasn't my best one.

Eve – It bombed.

Alan – Very kind of you to remind me…

Eve – I told you it needed a different title… And you killed him for that? Because he told you he didn't like a play that everyone thought was shitty?

Alan – I think it rekindled the rivalry we've had for years. Patrick and I have always competed—for everything, including girls. I remember once in secondary school…

Eve – Whatever. What happened?

Alan – It came to blows. He slipped and hit his head on a corner of the table.

Eve – The amount of blood on his shirt would indicate a sharp object was involved, rather than blunt force trauma.

Alan – Blood was pouring out of every orifice. Eyes, nose, ears. He convulsed for 15 minutes at least. And then nothing.

Eve – And you didn't think you should call 999?

Alan – You know what it's like, I say 15 minutes but maybe it was just a few minutes or even a few seconds, who knows. I was panicked. I froze. I didn't realise what was happening. When I decided to call for help, it was already too late… (*The doorbell rings. Alan looks worried.*) You think that's them now?

Eve – Who? The ambulance?

Alan – The police!

Eve – If you didn't call them…

Alan – The neighbours might have heard something.

Eve – Oh wait, it must be Emma…

Alan – Emma? Patrick's wife? How would she already know?

Eve – She doesn't know. She called me an hour ago. I completely forgot. She said she wanted to talk to me about something important. I told her to stop by…

Alan – We shouldn't let her in.

Eve – She's going to find that strange. I told her I'd be home.

Alan – You're right… OK, you answer the door. I'll hide in the kitchen.

Eve – We should tell her everything, don't you think? Get it over with…

Alan – Tell her what? That the body of her husband is lying on the kitchen floor in a pool of blood? Do you really think it's the best way to break it to her that she's a widow?

The doorbell rings again.

Eve – OK, I won't be long, we'll figure it out after.

Alan – Just make sure she doesn't come in the kitchen.

Alan goes to hide in the kitchen. Eve goes to the front door, after tucking the shirt back under the cushion.

Eve – Coming!

Eve returns with Emma.

Emma – I'm sorry to drop by at such short notice. Patrick isn't here, is he?

Eve – Patrick? Why on Earth would he… no, why?

Emma – I thought I saw his bike downstairs, never mind. Nothing looks more like a bike than another bike, don't you think?

Eve – Yes… Sure…

Emma – And Alan?

Eve – Yes, yes, he's here, but… he's working. On his new play. And you know him, when he's writing…

Emma – I understand… Especially since his last play was such a failure… What was it called again?

Eve – *Hiroshima.*

Emma – That's right. No wonder it bombed.

Eve – Surely that's not what you wanted to talk to me about…

Emma – I'm really sorry to bother you. I know it's not the right time, but it's important.

Eve – But of course! It's no bother at all, that's what friends are for… Do you want something to drink?

Emma – No thank you… I'm OK…

Eve – Good… *(Emma looks at her, surprised.)* No, I mean… Please, sit down… *(Emma is about to sit on the sofa, next to the cushion hiding the shirt.)* Err… no, why don't you sit over there.

Eve points Emma to a stool or a low bean bag that looks uncomfortable.

Emma *(sitting down)* – OK…

Eve – It's just that, these sofas, you know what they're like… It's easy to fall asleep. I'm a little tired and… I want to be really present for you… *(She grabs a seat similar to Emma's and sits down.)* So, what is it that you wanted to tell me that's so important?

Emma – So… You're not going to believe this… I just found out Patrick was cheating on me.

Eve – Really? And you didn't know?

Emma – Well… no. Why, did you?

Eve – But of course not! I mean… And do you know who with?

Emma – Not really.

Eve – Oh good, that's good…

Emma – What do you mean, good?

Eve – No, I mean, wouldn't it be worse if you knew who it was?

Emma – I don't know…

Eve – And it doesn't even really matter, right? What matters is that he's cheating on you.

Emma – Yes… Well yes, you're right. But it would be worse if he cheated with someone I know.

Eve – Yeah…

Emma – Can you imagine? Finding out your husband is cheating on you with your best friend?

Eve – What? What are you talking about…?

Emma – No, don't worry. I could never do that to you.

Eve – Thank you.

Emma – So anyway, it's over. I'm divorcing him.

Eve – Hang on, wait a minute… Isn't it a little early to make such a decision? Maybe it was an accident…

Emma – An accident? What do you mean? Do you think people hit on each other by mistake? Absentmindedly? And when things get hot and heavy, they just call the insurance company and let them sort it out?

Eve – No, of course not, but…

Emma – And then, when he comes home, the guy casually says to his wife: oh, by the way, I meant to tell you, I had a little accident, I rear-ended the neighbour's wife.

Eve – He rear-ended the neighbour's wife?

Emma – No, but I'm just saying! It's an example. Are you sure you're OK? This story seems to be upsetting you more than me.

Eve – I'm worried about you. As a couple you were so… When we said Patrick and Emma, it was…

Emma – Like saying Alan and Eve.

Eve – So now when you tell me you're breaking up…

Emma – Goes to show… Nothing lasts forever.

Eve – That's true, even Adam and Eve couldn't get their happy ever after.

Emma – Well, in any case, I'm never sleeping under the same roof as that bastard ever again.

Eve – I understand, of course…

Emma – And I can count on you for my divorce, right?

Eve – Are you sure? I don't know if… I'm friends with you both, it could become awkward.

Emma – Are you kidding? You're my friend! Patrick is more Alan's friend. We were friends long before we met them!

Eve – That's true…

Emma – Animals, every last one of them… Well, not Alan of course.

Eve – For sure.

Emma – Although, they are two sides of the same coin, you know…

Eve – Come on… Not all men… I assure you that Alan …

Emma – Oh just you wait, when I serve him the divorce papers he won't know what hit him. After all, you're a killer, right?

Eve – Pardon?

Emma – As a lawyer! You're a killer, aren't you? At least, that's your reputation.

Eve – It is?

Emma – Paloma told me. You know, you handled her divorce.

Eve – I did?

Emma – Yes, remember? She was married to a dentist. Big practice in Belgravia. Apparently, dental work was only one of the reasons his patients opened their mouths. Anyway, long story short, apparently you left him with nothing.

Eve – That's an exaggeration… And that's not what lawyers are for, you know… A divorce is first and foremost the failure of a life partnership. Lawyers are there to make the separation less painful…

Emma – Come on, don't be so modest. I know you're a killer. And let me tell you, I want you to bleed Patrick dry.

Alan returns, wearing a blood-stained apron.

Alan – Hello.

Emma – I thought you were writing your next successful play?

Alan – I was also doing some cooking at the same time…

Emma – Really…

Alan – Fun fact, writing and cooking have a lot in common… Both require good ingredients. A proven recipe. A little salt. A little spice. Then you let it simmer…

Emma – I see… I didn't know you were a foodie as well… What's your signature dish?

Alan – Deer burgers.

Eve – His famous secret recipe. No one's allowed in the kitchen when he's preparing it.

Alan – And you, how are you?

Eve – Patrick is no longer with us… I mean, Emma… She's no longer with Patrick…

Alan – No?

Emma – I just found out the bastard was cheating on me. Did you know anything about it?

Alan – Me? But of course not! Why would I know anything about it?

Emma – Bros before hos, don't think I don't know what it's like. Always ready to provide an alibi. Or a guest room…

Alan – I promise, Emma, it wasn't like that… Come on! We're friends. How can you think that I…

Emma – I'm sorry, I'm letting the emotions get the better of me… I don't know what I'm saying anymore.

Eve – Do you want to stay here for a bit, until you feel good enough to go home? And we can talk again in the morning, with clear heads. What do you think?

Emma – Home? I told you, it's out of the question! Actually, since you're both here, I want to ask you a favour…

Alan – Yes…?

Emma – Would you mind if I slept here tonight?

Eve – Well…

Emma – I'll find a solution tomorrow… Or I'll go and stay with my mother. But tonight, right now… (*She starts to sob*) I need to feel supported… And you're my only friends…

Eve walks towards her to give her a hug.

Eve – Yes, of course …

Emma – I knew I could count on you… I can't face talking to my mother right now. She hated Patrick. She always said he was a womaniser. Unfortunately, she was right, of course. But I can't bear her preaching to me right now. But with you…

Eve – But of course, we're here for you. Aren't we, Alan?

Emma – You're true friends. It means so much to me…

Emma leans into Eve for a hug.

Eve – Don't worry about it… It's not that bad… Well, I hope it isn't…

Alan – Right, I'll leave you girls to it, that deer meat isn't going to grind itself…

Eve watches him leave, horrified.

Emma – I swear, if he was standing right there in front of me, I don't think I could control myself… I'm having burger meat fantasies of my own right now. Fucking animal.

Eve – Come on, don't say that…

Emma (*wiping her tears*) – I am so sorry to drag you into this.

Eve – Are you feeling better?

Emma – A little… I think I'll take that drink now…

Eve – Err… Yes… What would you like?

Emma – A glass of tap water will be fine. Don't get up, I'll get it from the kitchen.

Eve – No!

Emma (*surprised*) – Oh right, I forgot… the secret recipe for the deer burgers.

Eve – You need something stronger, trust me.

Emma – I don't know if…

Eve – I'll have one with you. I need a drink too.

Emma – You do?

Eve removes a bottle and two glasses from a cabinet. She fills the glasses and raises hers for a toast.

Eve – We're stronger than that, aren't we? (*Breaking down*) We'll get through this…

She bursts into tears and now it's Emma's turn to walk towards her to console her.

Emma – I knew you were a friend but I really had no idea it would affect you that much…

Eve gets a hold of herself.

Eve – Let's toast. It won't make Patrick come back but we'll feel less tense.

She empties her glass in one gulp. Emma decides to do the same.

Emma – Wow… Strong enough to raise the dead…

Eve – If only…

Emma – What is it?

Eve – Potato liqueur.

Emma – Oh yes, it's… We can really taste the… Actually, it doesn't taste of anything, does it?

Eve – No.

Emma – But it does clear out the old airways…

Eve (*absentmindedly*) – Yes…

Silence.

Emma – How could I have been so fucking stupid…?

Eve – Pardon?

Emma – With Patrick! I didn't see anything coming…

Eve – He might come back… Maybe this is all just a nightmare, any moment now we'll all wake up.

Emma – I really don't think so… Remember when you asked me if I knew who it was?

Eve – Who?

Emma – The one Patrick cheated with!

Eve – Oh yes, and do you?

Emma – More like who they are…

Eve – How do you mean?

Emma – I guessed the password for his so-called work laptop, and I accidentally stumbled on his dating site account…

Eve – A dating site…?

Emma – TwoNightStands.com… He's not cheating on me with a woman, Eve, but with hundreds of them!

Eve – No?

Emma – He's a full-on sex addict, I tell you. Old ones, young ones, fat ones, thin ones, blondes, brunettes… He's not picky, that's for sure. Anything in a skirt.

Eve – Really…?

Emma – I am discovering a whole new side to him… And their pussies…

Eve – Oh because he also takes pictures of…

Emma – No, I mean… their cats. On their profile pictures. They all have cats. He hates cats.

Eve – Of course. That would be too far, there are limits, after all.

Emma – Yeah well, Patrick's pushed the limits so far they're more like a horizon.

Eve – Really?

Emma – You should see his chat history… Good grief… I'm not joking when I say I'm discovering a whole new side to him. Because with me, it was always rather plain vanilla…

Eve – Yes, with me as well… I mean, with Alan.

Emma – You should be careful. You think you know them, and then one day…

We hear the sound of an electric knife, or hedge trimmer, or chain saw…

Eve – He's trimming the hedges…

Emma – For the garnish?

The sound increases in volume and intensity.

Eve – Maybe I should go and have a look… I'll let you find the guest room…

Emma – Of course. Don't worry, I know the way… Thanks again, for everything.

Emma leaves. Alan returns.

Alan – Where did she go?

Eve – I strangled her and dumped the body in the tub until we decide what to do next. Might as well get rid of all annoying witnesses.

Alan – You didn't?

Eve – Of course not! What about you? What on earth is going on? What's all this noise?

Alan – I couldn't leave him in the middle of the kitchen floor.

Eve – So what did you do?

Alan – I stuffed him in the freezer. Just until we decide what we want to do with the body.

Eve – And then you decided to do some yard work? In the kitchen?

Alan – No, but… He wouldn't fit in one piece…

Eve – Oh dear God… I can't believe this… How did we get here, Alan? That's it, I'm calling the cops.

She takes out her mobile.

Alan – Do you want to send me to prison?

Eve – That's where criminals belong, isn't it?

Alan – But I keep telling you, it was an accident.

She changes her mind.

Eve – Are you sure he's dead?

Alan – Do you mean, am I sure he was really dead before I cut him in three pieces with the hedge trimmer?

Eve – I'll take "Things I Ever thought I'd hear from the man I married", Alex.

Alan – Remember our vows… For better or for worse… You should have thought about that before.

Eve – Before what?

Alan – Before cheating on me with Patrick…

Eve – You've lost your mind, Alan. You need help. You said so yourself, it was involuntary manslaughter. We'll plead temporary insanity.

Eve calls the police.

Alan – Don't do that…

Eve – It's the only solution, trust me.

Alan – You'll be charged as an accomplice.

Eve – How so?

Alan – His wife is here and you haven't told her anything.

Eve – But why would I have helped you kill him?

Alan – Because he was cheating on you too! You wanted revenge.

Eve – What do you mean, he cheated on me?

Alan – I overheard you talking earlier. I knew about his account on that website…

Eve – So you knew everything?

Alan – You know, when it comes to getting laid, men like to brag… Makes you wonder if they don't cheat on their wives just so they can boast about it with their friends. Must be their hunter-gatherer instinct: hunt the women then gather round with their friends to swap stories.

Eve – And you didn't tell me?

Alan – Why would you need to know? It would only have made you uncomfortable with Emma…

Eve – I see, so you wanted to protect me. Regardless, that doesn't give me a reason to kill Patrick.

Alan – Really…?

Eve – Why would I have killed him?

Alan – Jealousy, of course. Just like Emma…

Eve – What are you talking about now…

Alan – You thought you were the only one. You couldn't bear the idea that you were just one among many. And when I told you I wanted to kill him, you offered to help. With him dead, there would be no trace of your transgression.

Eve – You are completely out of your mind, Alan!

Alan – We both are. Birds of a feather and all that. I can just picture the headlines: "Evil couple dismember best friend's husband's body and store it in freezer while dining with the widow in the next room".

Eve – You're not thinking of telling that version of the story to the police, are you? Just to drag me along with you? It's monstrous!

Alan – But I won't have to say anything! That's what the judge will think. Even if I maintain that I was acting alone, he'll think I'm trying to protect you.

She seems uncertain.

Eve – You think?

Alan – Either way, it'll be the end of your career. No one will want their divorce handled by someone who dismembers her lovers with a hedge trimmer.

Eve – Unfortunately, you have a point…

Alan – And don't forget the part where you'll have to tell the judge that you cheated on me involuntarily.

Eve – But that part's true, I swear!

Alan – Involuntary adultery? Run it by me, see if you can convince me…

Eve – It was that weekend where you were in Liverpool for the premiere of *Hiroshima*, actually. I had to drive to Brighton to be in court, but the trial got postponed.

Alan – You can just say that you didn't want to witness the flop in person…

Eve – Either way, we were both meant to be away. So the house was supposed to be empty.

Alan – Patrick had asked me for my keys, so he would have somewhere to take one of his lovers. So it was you?

Eve – Of course not! I came home during the night. I didn't know you had let him use the house… and our marital bed, to shag one of his floozies!

Alan – It's the only double bed in the house… So?

Eve – So I went to bed immediately after coming home.

Alan – With Patrick…

Eve – I knew there was someone in the bed, but I thought it was you! I thought maybe you decided to come home right after the play ended. I knew it would flop so I wasn't surprised…

Alan – Thank you for the vote of no confidence…

Eve – I was very quiet, I didn't want to wake you up.

Alan – But in the end your partner woke up nonetheless.

Eve – Patrick's tart left at some point during the night. And apparently, he was ready for seconds.

Alan – So you were subbed in, is that it? You came in at half time…

Emma – He must have thought I was her. It's only the next morning that I realised he wasn't you. Although, I did think something was off.

Alan – Why, because it was better?

Eve – Of course not… Let's just say it was different… And I couldn't figure out why you insisted on calling me Alexandra69.

Alan – He pulled out all the stops, is that it?

Eve – It's just that… I forgot what it was like…

Alan – Go on, add insult to injury…

Emma returns.

Emma – I'm sorry… Could you lend me a toothbrush? I left in such a hurry. I hadn't planned…

Alan – Sure, just remember, try not to jump in the wrong bed tonight… You never know…

Emma – Err, sure…

Alan – I'll leave you to it… You must have lots to talk about… Compare notes…

He leaves.

Emma – Whatever did he mean?

Eve – I have no idea… Actually, I do…

Emma – What?

Eve – He's accusing me of cheating on him.

Emma – And… is it true?

Eve – It was… an involuntary adultery.

Emma – Involuntary adultery…? Is that a joke?

Eve – No.

Emma – Okay…

Eve – I came home one night. There was a man in my bed. It's only the next morning that I realised it wasn't my husband.

Emma – Are you fucking kidding me?

Eve – Absolutely not.

Emma – Eve, no one is going to believe this. Certainly not your husband…

Eve – You're right. It's totally unrealistic.

Emma – It's shame, though. Can you imagine? Guilt-free pleasure.

Eve – And without consequences…

Emma – Was is worth it?

Eve – I…

Emma – Cheating without knowing, is not really cheating. *(They both burst into nervous laughter, but Emma stops abruptly.)* But… if Patrick ever told me a story that stupid he'd really be taking me for a fucking idiot…

Eve – Yes, of course… But… Don't you think that part of being a couple means being able to forgive the other person?

Emma – Forgive? I'd kill him, believe me.

Eve – A figure of speech, I imagine.

Emma – You've never wanted to kill someone?

Eve – Well…

Emma – If Alan cheated on you, for example, could you kill him?

Eve – Why? Do you know something I don't?

Emma – No, no, of course not…

Eve – So… you've never cheated on Patrick then?

Emma – No… Well… That depends on what you mean by cheating.

Eve – Is that so?

Emma – I mean, technically…

Eve – I see… Do blowjobs count, that kind of thing… ?

Alan returns.

Alan – It'll be a few minutes. I spilled the beans.

Eve – Spilled the beans? So you've decided to confess everything?

Alan – No, I meant the beans for dinner…

Emma – Oh, that's right… the deer burgers…

Eve – I'll go freshen up…

Eve leaves. Embarrassed silence.

Emma – You didn't tell her?

Alan – Tell her what?

Emma – Our little indiscretion, on New Years Eve.

Alan – But of course not! Why do you ask?

Emma – I don't know… She's acting weird…

Alan – That's not why, don't worry about it.

Emma – No, but because we've never spoken about it… I was a little drunk. You too… It didn't mean anything, right? It was just… an accident.

Alan – Oh, not you as well… What it is with you both and your accidents…

Emma – I'm sorry for bringing it up, I shouldn't have…

Alan – Don't worry, it's already forgotten…

Eve returns, looking a little out of sorts.

Eve – So, let's eat this deer then.

The doorbell rings.

Alan – Who could that be…?

Eve – The police?

Emma, puzzled by their strange behaviour, looks at them, worried.

Alan – I'll get it… If I'm not back in five minutes, call my lawyer…

Eve glances at Emma with a meaningful look, to reassure her.

Eve – A private joke.

Emma – OK…

Eve – Do you like deer meat?

Emma – Yes, well…

Alan returns with a package.

Alan – It's the sushi delivery.

Eve – Oh right, I completely forgot.

Emma – You ordered sushi as well?

Embarrassed silence.

Black.

Act 2

E m m a – Your burgers are really excellent, Alan. Congratulations.

Alan – Thank you… I apologise for the lead shot that almost broke your tooth. It doesn't matter how careful you are picking them out, there's always a couple left.

Emma – It's not that easy to remove all trace of a crime, is it? I had no idea you were a hunter…

Eve – Me neither, actually…

Alan – Well, nowadays it's not something you brag about.

Emma – So you really killed this poor animal yourself?

Alan – Oh you know, I'm only starting out… I only have a small rifle.

Emma – Yes, that's very true…

Alan – No I mean, I use a small caliber. Nothing wrong with my rifle…

Emma – But a deer, that's quite a large animal. Don't you need a large caliber to shoot one?

Alan – Let's say it was more like… an accident.

Emma – An accident? Well, what do you know…

Alan – I was returning from a hunting trip where I didn't catch anything… With Patrick, actually. And on the way back this deer ran across the road, right under the car.

Emma – Maybe it was a suicidal deer. Looking to end its miserable stag life.

Alan – Yes, maybe…

Emma – You're really full of hot air…

Alan – Pardon?

Emma – No, I mean, you spend a lot of time outside, getting fresh air… hunting, golfing…

Eve – You play golf, too?

Alan – Yes, I've started playing again… a little…

Emma – And… do you actually play with Patrick, or are you just his alibi for when he's romping around with his nymphos?

Alan – No, no, we really play golf together, I promise. He's very good, actually…

Emma – Yes… And from what he tells me, the 18 holes in Epping Forest is worth the trip…

Eve – You should take me with you one of these days, Alan. I'd love to try a little golf, too.

Emma – And you'll have to give me that burger recipe. Oh no, that's right… that's also a secret.

Embarrassed silence.

Eve – Does anyone want more beans?

Emma – No thank you… really… I can't stomach anything else…

Alan – If you want to go and rest your head, don't mind us.

Emma – With everything that's happened I don't think I'll be able to sleep for a while… but it's nice to know that in these horrible times you can count on your friends.

Eve – Consider this your home, Emma…

Alan – Dessert, anyone?

Eve – We have Cornettos in the freezer…

Emma – Thank you, I'm fine… I'll go wash my hands, if I may…

She gets up.

Alan – Use the bathroom, the kitchen is rather messy…

She leaves. Alan helps himself to another burger.

Eve – Nice to see you taking this so well… I see it hasn't spoiled your appetite…

Alan – Starving myself to death wouldn't change anything.

Eve – Why did you tell her you were a hunter?

Alan – I don't know… It just came out. I had to find something to keep her from going in the kitchen.

Eve – And what's with these burgers? What are they made of? Or is it better if I don't ask…?

Alan – No, no… That's really deer meat… Organic, free-range deer meat…

Eve – Also, we'll have to talk about this golf thing later, because it sounds fishy to me…

Alan – Of course, I have nothing to hide…

Eve – Except for a body… So I'll ask you one more time: is this a joke? Because if it is, it's in really poor taste. May I remind you that the widow is in the room next door.

Alan – Go check in the freezer yourself if you want. But be warned: it's not a pretty sight.

Eve – You're right… See no evil… Hear no evil…

Alan – You won't be able to say you didn't see or hear anything… We're not talking about frozen babies, shoved among Tupperware of frozen leftovers. This is a 6-foot-tall man split in three 2-foot segments …

Eve – You're a monster… Preventing the lawful burial of a body, do you know what that gets you? Do you want me to spend the best years of my life in prison?

Alan – Mutually assured destruction, Eve. If I fall, you fall. You have to help me!

Emma returns.

Emma – I'm going to call him.

Eve – I don't think that's a good idea.

Emma – I'm going to have break up with him at some point!

Eve – You sure you don't want to think about it a little longer?

Emma – All the thinking's been done. I'll never forgive him for what he did to me.

Alan – Sure, but talking to him can wait until tomorrow, no?

Emma – If I don't come home tonight, he's going to wonder what happened. He might even call the police.

Eve – Ah yes, in that case… Maybe you should let him know.

Alan – Given the state he's in I don't think he'll call the police, but sure…

Emma – The state he's in?

Alan – I mean… He might already suspect that you know, and feel uncomfortable about the situation.

Eve – Don't you think it'd be better if you went home? Tomorrow is another day…

Emma – I'll never be able to sleep under the same roof as this mother fucker again.

Eve – You think you're in the right state of mind to talk to him?

Emma – Look, I'm not going to discuss how we split our assets or who gets custody of the dog. I just want to tell him to contact my lawyer. Aka you.

Alan – Oh, so you're going to handle their divorce?

Eve – I don't know… Yes… Emma asked me…

Alan – Right… So if you insist on calling him now… do you want to be left alone?

Eve – If you want, you call him from the…

Alan – Not the kitchen.

Emma – You don't have to leave, I'd like you to stay actually.

She calls Patrick on her mobile. We hear a phone ringing in the next room.

Emma – That's weird, it sounds like it's ringing next door…

Alan – Must be mine.

Emma – Aren't you going to get it?

Alan – Yes, yes, sure…

He leaves, Eve gives him a puzzled look.

Emma – He's not picking up…

Eve – Well… I'm not surprised.

Emma – Why do you say that?

Eve – If he saw you were calling, and if he knows why you're calling him, and… he probably isn't going to pick up.

Emma – It's him… Patrick? I know everything. What do you think? Oh please, don't pretend you don't know what I'm talking about. Yes, your 18th hole, that's right. What's your username on TwoNightStands.com again? Oh yes, Patrick327. Hard to believe there are 326 other mother fuckers with the same loser first name. You piece of shit! Is that all you have to say? You little fucker. It's over, Patrick327. Next time you want to talk to me, talk to my lawyer. And guess what? You've already met her, it's Eve. Yes, Eve! That's right, Alan's wife, your best mate. Didn't see that one coming, did you? Have a good night, you piece of shit! *(She puts her mobile away.)* Right, that's done. I feel better now I got it all out…

Eve is aghast.

Eve – Who was that?

Emma – What do you mean, who was that? Him! Who do you think?

Eve – Patrick? What did he say?

Emma – Not very much, actually. What could he say? He sounded strange. I think I'm going to take an aspirin… I feel a headache coming on… Can I get a glass of water from the bathroom?

Eve – Of course.

Emma – Bastard…

Emma leaves. Alan returns.

Alan – Are you OK? What happened?

Eve – You really took me for a ride, didn't you?

Alan – What?

Eve – Emma. She just spoke to Patrick on the phone.

Alan – It was me.

Eve – What?

Alan – Patrick's mobile! It was in his pocket so of course, it's still there now… I picked up when she called, to avoid raising suspicions…

Eve – Really? So that's why she said he had a strange voice.

Alan – I did like they do on the telly. I covered the speaker with a handkerchief.

Eve – You are certifiably insane…

Alan – But now we have an alibi. I couldn't have killed him an hour ago if she just spoke to him on the phone.

Eve – Unless the police decide to trace the location of the call and find that it came from our kitchen.

Alan – Do you think they'll look that closely?

Eve – This is a serious crime. They might.

Silence. Alan pretends to be on the verge of tears.

Alan – If you knew how much I'm sorry… If only I could go back in time, just an hour… Unfortunately that's not possible…

Eve – Did you really kill him because he didn't like your play?

A beat.

Alan – Yes… Among other things…

Eve – What other things?

A beat.

Alan – He told me he slept with you.

Eve – I see… Why didn't you tell me before?

Alan – I wanted to see if you would tell me first…

Eve – So you didn't believe him either when he told you it was a misunderstanding.

Alan – He didn't tell me it was a misunderstanding. That's the problem…

Eve – Mother fucker… I'm going to kill him!

Alan – I've already done that… I'm only asking you to help me get rid of the body. If you love me… Do you love me?

Eve – Of course I love you. How do you not know that?

Alan – I do know that.

Eve – What about me? Do you believe me, that I slept with him by mistake?

Alan – I'm trying… You have to agree that's more difficult…

Eve – What can I do to prove how much I love you…

Alan – You've already done enough. But you're right, there is zero chance of me not going to prison. And I don't want to be the reason you're going down with me. I'll call the police.

Eve – No, wait!

Alan – What?

Eve – I don't want you to go to prison for years and years.

Alan – So what do we do?

Eve – I'll help you get rid of Patrick…

Alan – How do we do that?

Eve – You know, as a lawyer, I've had many clients share trade secrets with me over the years. Including a few foolproof ways to fit a six-foot-long body through the drain of a bath tub, after a night soaking in a bath of acid.

Alan – I see…

Eve – But first we have to get rid of her.

Alan – Get rid of her?

Eve – She can't be here running around!

Alan – Oh, you scared me…

Emma returns.

Emma – What's with the faces? Is there a problem?

Eve – No, no, of course not.

Emma – I tried lying down a bit, but I can't sleep.

Alan – How about we open a bottle of something to take the edge off?

Emma – I don't know if I can, I just took some pills… I don't think you can mix them?

Eve – Come on, one small drink after dinner never hurt anyone.

Emma – You know what, why not? It'll help digest the deer… Tasty, but a little rich, no?

Eve pours three glasses and discretely slips a pill in one of them.

Alan – Oh, you're going for the lighter fluid again, good choice…

Emma – Potato liqueur…

Eve – A specialty from Sodgibbon.

Emma – Sodgibbon?

Alan – Eve has an uncle there. A man of the cloth. He distills it at night in the illegal still he setup in the church crypt.

Emma, miles away, isn't really listening.

Emma – I wonder where he could have met his lovers.

Alan – There's plenty of hotels everywhere.

Emma – He was so stingy. I doubt it. In fact, I'm certain he used that site only so he wouldn't have to pay for prozzies. Because trust me, I saw the pictures of his bimbos, clearly he wasn't going for their looks…

Eve – Thanks…

Emma looks at her, intrigued.

Alan – Why did you use the past tense?

Emma – Pardon?

Eve – You said: he was so stingy.

Emma – Because he's dead to me.

Eve – Come on, don't say that…

Emma – Either that, or he had a friend who let him use his flat… Men are quick to have each other's backs in those cases, aren't they. Present company excepted, of course, Alan…

Alan tops her glass.

Alan – Come on, stop thinking about it… Have another drink instead.

Emma – I don't know what's… Just a few moments ago I couldn't sleep, but now I'm crashing… I think I'll go lie down…

She falls to the ground.

Alan – Looks like the headache pills kicked in, in the end…

Eve – More like the sleeping pill I spiked her drink with.

Alan – You didn't…?

Eve – Now we have all the time we need to get rid of the body.

Alan – Hers?

Eve – No, Patrick's! Help me take her to the guest room. She's going to sleep until tomorrow morning and when she wakes up, she'll be officially widowed.

Alan – We even spared her the complications of a nasty divorce.

Eve – So really, we're doing her a favour.

They drag her by her feet backstage and return immediately.

Alan – And for Patrick, what do we do?

Eve – A tub full of acid will take too long.

Alan – Especially if Emma wants to take a shower tomorrow morning…

Eve – You're right…

Alan – We'll bag Patrick in three bin bags. And we'll take him for a walk in the forest…

Eve – Or a zoo. I saw that in a film once… We throw him in the lion's enclosure and Bob's your uncle.

Alan – How do you propose we walk past security at London Zoo with three large bin bags?

Eve – We could take him at night?

Alan – Hampstead Heath will do just fine. I have a shovel in the shed outside.

Eve – And for… Patrick, do you want help?

Alan – I've already done most of it, I'll finish it. It's just too messy…

Eve – As you wish…

He leaves.

Eve – I hope I'm not making a mistake… Anyway… it's too late now. Another one, for the road…

She pours herself another glass and gulps it down. Her mobile rings.

Eve – Hello… (*Stunned*) Patrick? If this is a joke it's really not funny. Is that you Alan? Sorry Patrick, is that really you? No, no, of course I'm not surprised, but… Well, a little actually… Oh, you left your mobile here. Yes, he told me about your… discussion. But why did you have to go and tell him? Anyway, now it's done… I guess he had to know, eventually… OK, I'll tell him… Right. Thanks for calling. By the way, have you spoken with Emma? Yes, I think she may suspect something. Yes, something like that… OK, bye Patrick… (*She hangs up.*) Mother fucker… He really had me going…

Alan returns with bulging bin bags.

Eve (*not giving anything away*) – So, that's it? It's done?

Alan – Yes. Took me longer than I thought, the frozen pieces had started to stick to the sides of the freezer… I had to use an ice pick…

Eve – Poor Patrick… I'm feeling all sorts of emotions seeing him like that, bundled like the recycling on pick up day…

Alan – I don't know how to thank you. This is an incredible proof of love.

Eve – Does that mean I am forgiven for this involuntary adultery?

Alan – Of course… You've showed me how much you love me.

Eve – And I forgive you for putting our best friend in my bed without telling me, OK?

Alan – There's two more bags.

Eve – I'll help you…

Alan – Are you sure?

Eve – For better or for worse… remember?

They leave. Emma enters, in a trance.

Emma – Is anyone here? Where did I put my phone?

She looks at the bin bags with curiosity. Looking for her mobile, she lifts a cushion on the sofa and finds the shirt covered in blood with cufflinks… Intrigued, she slowly comes out of her torpor. She opens one of the bin bags and closes it immediately, horrified… The other two arrive with two more bags.

Alan – Emma, what are you doing here?

Eve – I thought you were asleep?

Emma – No… I mean, yes… I just came looking for my mobile…

Alan – We were just taking the rubbish out…

Emma – I'm going back to bed. Don't mind me…

She leaves, visibly scared.

Alan – You think she suspects something?

Eve – Maybe we should wack her off too?

Alan – I didn't know you were ready to kill for me. I'm almost scared…

Eve (*exhilarated*) – You know that Tammy Wynette song? *Stand by your man*! (*Singing*) Doin' things that you don't understand. But if you love him you'll forgive him. Even though he's hard to understand.

Alan (*worried*) – Listen, I need to tell you something…

Eve – Don't tell me you killed someone else!

Alan – No, that's the thing… I mean, yes, but…

Eve – Poor Patrick… He was a friend, you know. I'd like to say one last goodbye. Which bag is the head in?

Alan – I wouldn't do that if I were you…

Eve – I think we need to talk, don't you think…?

Alan – OK, it's not Patrick in the bin bags.

Eve – What do you mean, not Patrick? You killed someone else?

Alan – No, I mean, I didn't kill anyone… How could you even believe such a thing?

Eve – I don't know what I believe anymore… *(She opens one of the bags and her smile freezes.)* No… This is horrific… So you really killed someone?

Alan – Of course not! I mean yes, but…

Eve – What's this I'm looking at?

Alan – The deer…

Eve – The deer? But Alan, you're not a hunter… Or is that another thing you kept from me?

Alan – I don't hunt, don't worry. But the story about the deer, that's true.

Eve – No kidding… I'd love to hear it…

Alan – I was with Patrick, actually. We had just finished playing golf.

Eve – Oh yes, golf, I forgot… Let me guess, somewhere between the seventeenth and the eighteenth hole, you killed a deer with a golf ball?

Alan – We were on our way home. As we drove through Epping Forest, we hit a deer. We almost died, if you must know. Because hitting a 200-pound animal at sixty miles an hour causes a lot of damage even when you're driving a large 4x4.

Eve – Yes, I can imagine…

Alan – We ended in the ditch… Patrick had a mild concussion.

Eve – And then?

Alan – Since he was still alive, I decided to take him to the vet.

Eve – Patrick?

Alan – The deer! We put him in the boot. But when we got to the vet, he had died of his wounds.

Eve – Who?

Alan – The deer!

Eve – Oh, right…

Alan – Since he was already in the car, we didn't know what to do with him. That's when Patrick had the idea to turn it into mince…

Eve – A great idea… But why this whole rigmarole?

Alan – While we were cutting it up, Patrick confessed that he slept with you…

Eve – Clearly something must have inspired him as he was butchering the deer… And what did he tell you? Because unlike me, he knew he was in his best friend's bed.

Alan – Yes, that's why he was feeling guilty. It was weighing on his conscience.

Eve – His conscience? Patrick?

Alan – You're right, looking back I think he may have just wanted to humiliate me… All the while hiding behind the fact that it was an involuntary adultery… like you say.

Eve – And then?

Alan – Eventually he admitted he knew exactly what he was doing… and that in all probability, so did you…

Eve – The bastard… I swear that…

Alan – Anyway, it came to blows.

Eve – So the blood on your shirt…

Alan – No, that's the deer, when we put him in the boot…

Eve – I see…

Alan – Then we made up. I gave him one of my shirts and he left.

Eve – And then?

Alan – When you came home, I was angry at you. Because you hadn't told me. I felt betrayed. Cheated.

Eve – I'm sorry. But I swear that I didn't know that he…

Alan – That's when I had an idea. It just popped in my head. Cutting up this poor animal made me lose my sense of reality. I found a recipe in Woman's Own.

Eve – Woman's Own?

Alan – To get back at you. I told you I killed him. To see how you'd react. After that, one thing lead to another…

We hear a police siren. Eve sees the shirt sticking out from one of the bin bags.

Eve – Emma… She saw the bags and the shirt… She must have called the police…

Someone knocks violently on the door. Emma enters, holding a large knife.

Emma – Don't come near me, bunch of sickos…

Eve – Calm down, we can explain. It was just a stupid joke…

Alan – It's okay, it's not Patrick in the bin bags.

Emma – Don't move, or I shoot!

Alan – That's a knife…

Eve – Let me open one, look, you can see for yourself.

She shows her the contents of one of the bin bags.

Emma – Oh my God, what is that?

Alan – It's a deer! Look! All that hair.

Emma – Patrick also had a lot of hair!

Eve – Not that much…

Emma – How would you know?

Off – Police!

Alan – You called them, it's best if you talk to them.

Eve – It might be tricky…

Emma – OK…

Emma leaves.

Alan – I'm sorry. I was stupid. But I felt betrayed…

Eve – It's my fault… I should have told you right after it happened. But I didn't think you'd believe me, you know…

Alan – We were both foolish.

Eve – Goes to show, sweeping things under the carpet is never a good solution… It always comes back blowing in your face…

Alan – Agreed. That's why you should also tell her.

Eve – Who?

Alan – Emma! For Patrick.

Eve – It doesn't matter, he cheats on her with anything in a skirt.

Alan – Yes, but you're her best friend…

Emma returns.

Emma – Everything's sorted, they're gone. I'm sorry, I don't know what took me.

Eve – We're all a little confused, tonight… It must be the full moon…

Emma – I didn't know it was a full moon.

Eve – If it isn't, it sure feels like it should be.

Alan – I'll leave you to it, I think you have things to talk about…

Alan leaves.

Emma – What does he mean?

A beat.

Eve – I slept with Patrick.

Emma – What?

Eve – I swear, it was… totally involuntary.

Emma – So that story you told me earlier, that was you… and Patrick?

Eve – I wanted to tell you for a while, but I didn't know how.

Emma – But how is that even possible?

Eve – Alan, that bastard, let him use our marital bed for his trysts…

Emma – Yes, that makes sense… And I don't want to know more… You're my best friend after all, right?

Eve – Thank you, Emma.

Emma – We all make mistakes, especially when we've had too much to drink.

Eve – I was stone cold sober.

Emma – Yes well, that's not the point. Patrick is the bastard here. Good thing he's not in my field of vision right now, I could actually kill him!

Eve – Don't worry, you don't just up and kill someone… But if you need a lawyer, I'm here for you… For your divorce, I mean…

Emma – Thank you… Right, I think I better go. You must have things to talk about, too… I'll spend the night at my mother's. I'll tell her I locked myself out.

Eve – Take care of yourself… Tomorrow is another day… For everyone…

Emma leaves. Alan returns. They sit on the sofa and remain silent for a while.

Alan – Was it really involuntary?

Eve – Let's say… voluntarily involuntary, then.

Alan – Alright, I'll pretend to believe you.

They embrace.

Eve – On the plus side, my sex drive got a boost…

Alan – Yes, I noticed. I wonder what it was.

Eve – We should do this more often.

Alan – Do what? More blind dates in our marital bed…?

Eve – Why? Do you have other friends who come to our flat for their sleazy hookups?

Alan – I was thinking the other way around. You must have friends who cheat on their husbands… I'm one behind, not that anyone's counting…

Eve – Sorry, all my friends are faithful…

They kiss.

Black.

Epilog

Three suitcases are lined up against the wall in the living room. Alan comes in from the street, and removes his raincoat.

Alan – Honey! Are you there?

Eve arrives.

Eve – So, how'd it go?

Alan – They love the play. They want to setup a stage production after the summer holidays.

Eve – What? But that's amazing!

Alan – And they found the perfect title.

Eve – *An Innocent Little Murder*… Sounds better than *Hiroshima*, doesn't it?

Alan – Probably because it rings so true…

Eve – Almost…

They kiss.

Alan – So in the end, all is well that ends well.

Eve – I always believed in you… Even when your stories were obviously tall tales.

Alan – In the end, this ordeal has brought us closer together. I promise I'll never lie to you again.

Eve – And I promise I won't keep anything from you.

Alan notices the suitcases.

Alan *(worried)* – What's with the suitcases? Are you leaving me? After what you just said, I thought…

Eve – They're Emma's. She asked if she could spend the night here. I don't think it went very well with Patrick… She didn't have anywhere to go.

Alan – She's such a pain in the ass…

Eve – We owe her that much…

Alan – OK… But just for one night…

The doorbell rings.

Eve – That must be her…

Alan – OK, I'll get the champagne.

Eve – To celebrate Emma's divorce?

Alan – To celebrate my play finding a producer! We'll just have to celebrate with her.

Alan leaves. Eve goes to open the door and returns with Emma.

Eve – You don't look OK. Did you have an argument?

Emma – Listen, Eve… I think I made a big mistake…

Eve – You're scaring me, Emma… What kind of mistake?

Emma – I think I killed Patrick.

Eve – Come on, I've heard that one before. Try something else!

Emma – We had a talk, the two of us. It escalated quickly. I told him to leave the house immediately.

Eve – And then.

Emma – Then… well he went to pack his bags. That's when things sort of took a turn for the worse.

Eve – Sort of?

Emma – I was cutting a roast chicken… With a knife in my hand and … I got carried away.

Eve – Where is he? In hospital?

Emma – Unfortunately it was too late to get help. I just wanted to scare him. He stepped towards me to dare me. I raised my arm in a reflex and… I cut his carotid

Eve – Oh my God… The nightmare continues. So, but where is he?

Emma points to the suitcases with her eyes.

Emma – Err, well… In the suitcases…

Eve – No?

Emma – I'm going to be in need of your counsel, Eve.

Eve – My counsel? You mean as a lawyer? Don't get your hopes up, Emma. Even a killer lawyer like me… There's no way we can pass this for a household accident…

Emma – I was thinking more about passing it through the drain after a night in a bathtub full of acid…

Eve – I'm going to have to talk to Alan about this…

Alan returns, looking delighted, waiving a bottle of champagne.

Alan – Champagne!

The two women look at him, dumbstruck.

Black.

May 2020

9 782377 054428